Messy
Murray Brown

Colin West

Hodder
Children's
Books

A division of Hodder Headline plc

Copyright © 1995 Colin West

First published in Great Britain in 1995 by
Hodder Children's Books

This edition published as a My First Read Alone
in 1998 by Hodder Children's Books

The right of Colin West to be identified as the Author of the
Work has been asserted in accordance with the Copyright,
Designs and Patents Act 1988.

10 9 8 7 6 5 4 3

A catalogue record for this book is available from
the British Library

ISBN 0 340 72661 X

Printed and bound in Great Britain
by The Devonshire Press Ltd, Torquay, TQ2 7NX

Hodder Children's Books
A Division of Hodder Headline plc
338 Euston Road
London NW1 3BH

Chapter One

Mr and Mrs Brown lived in a tall
house with yellow shutters
and apple trees in the garden.

When they weren't at work,
Mr Brown did crosswords
and Mrs Brown made silk flowers.
Life might have been perfect for
them had it not been for their son,
Murray.

Murray Brown troubled
his parents.
His room was a mess.
His clothes were a mess.

His hair was a mess.
In short, Murray Brown was one
big sloppy mess.

Mr and Mrs Brown despaired of
their son.
"Do this!" they told him.

"Don't do that!" they implored him.
But Murray just didn't take any
notice.
Mr and Mrs Brown were at
their wits' end.

Chapter Two

One day, Mr Brown noticed an ad
in his paper, just above
the crossword.

"Just think of it - a cleaned-up-forever Murray!" sighed Mr Brown. "Let's try it!" said Mrs Brown.

So Mr and Mrs Brown sent off their seventy-seven pounds and waited for things to happen.

Days went by (during which time
Murray was as messy as ever).

At last, there was a knock at the
door, and standing there was
Dr Humphrey himself.
"Show me your messy child and
I'll clean him up forever!" he
announced.

Mr and Mrs Brown took the
doctor upstairs to meet Murray.
(It was nearly noon, but he was
still in bed.)

Dr Humphrey climbed over the
mess on the floor and cleared his
throat loudly.

Murray muttered something rude
and turned over.
Mr and Mrs Brown looked at
each other rather awkwardly.

"A typical case," said
Dr Humphrey. "It won't be easy,
but I'll do my best."

Mr and Mrs Brown smiled
gratefully.

They pulled Murray from his
messy bed and Dr Humphrey got
to work.

Dr Humphrey dangled a watch in front of Murray's eyes, and spoke in a slow, deliberate voice.

He scribbled things in a notebook
as Murray lay messily on the
couch.

Two hours later, Murray Brown
came out, looking different.
His once-messy clothes were tidy.
His once-messy face was clean.

Mr and Mrs Brown were
overjoyed.
"We've got a son to be proud of!"
they chortled, hugging each other.

Dr Humphrey shook them all by
the hand and gave them his card.
"Just call if you should need me
again," he said.
Then he left for his next
clean-up-forever appointment.

Chapter Three

Mr and Mrs Brown looked
proudly at their cleaned-up son.
Life would be perfect now!
"Let's show him off to the
neighbours!" they hooted.

They paraded down the High Street and introduced Murray to everyone they came across.

"I wish my son was as neat as yours!" said Mrs Dundee.

"My daughter could learn a thing or two from Murray," commented Mr Rudolph.

Mr and Mrs Brown beamed
with pride.

They walked round the block
sixteen times, then headed home.

At supper time, Murray behaved
perfectly.
He used a napkin.
He didn't pick his food.
He didn't talk with his mouth full.
He kept his elbows off the table.

He didn't ask for second helpings.
His table manners were
impeccable.

"Tomorrow we can show him off
to the family!" whispered Mr Brown.

Chapter Four

Next day, Murray was up early.
After he'd made his bed, pressed
his trousers and dusted his room,
Mr and Mrs Brown took him to
visit relations.

"Goodness me! How smart Murray
looks!" said Auntie Ethel and
Uncle Dan.

"If only our Alison was half as
tidy!" said Uncle Max to Aunty May.

Murray straightened a few pictures
and perched on the sofa.
When it was time to leave, Murray
said goodbye most politely and
wiped his feet on the way out.

As soon as the Brown family arrived home that evening, Murray started tidying the living room. He dusted all the furniture, ornaments and skirting board. "Tut tut," he muttered under his breath, "I've never seen such dirt."

Murray rearranged the chairs, plumped up the cushions, and then went up to tidy his room (although it was perfectly tidy already.)

Mr and Mrs Brown sat down for a
cup of cocoa.

"Everyone agrees Murray is neat,"
Mr Brown said.
"They certainly do," agreed
Mrs Brown.
They sipped their cocoa quietly
before going to bed.

Chapter Five

Next morning Murray was up
early again.
He had work to do.

"What's that noise?" asked Mr
Brown as he awoke with a start.
Mrs Brown sat up in bed.
"Sounds like a vacuum cleaner,"
she said.

She was right. Murray was
hoovering the stairs.

Next, they heard the rumbling of
the washing machine.

Then they heard the humming of
the dishwasher.

"It's not normal, you know," said
Mr Brown. "Kids shouldn't be neat
and tidy all the time. Kids are
meant to be messy."

Mrs Brown agreed.
"We've got the cleanest kid in town!"
she said. "Everyone must think
we're odd to raise such a son."

"We'll have to do something," they agreed. They dressed and rushed downstairs.

Murray was dusting the pot plants.
"Stop it Murray!" his parents
told him. "You needn't be neat all
the time. You can make a mess
like other kids."

Murray looked at them
in horror.
He didn't want to be messy.
He wanted to be neat and tidy for
the rest of his life.

49

Murray washed the curtains as his parents ranted.

And he scrubbed the floor as his
parents raved.

Then Murray polished the door
knobs, tidied the mantelpiece
and ironed the newspaper.
"I don't like unnecessary creases,"
he told them.

Suddenly Mrs Brown remembered
something: Dr Humphrey's
business card! She found it in the
bureau (where Murray had filed it
away neatly). Quickly she phoned
the doctor's number.

"Can you come over straight away?" she begged. "It's an emergency!"

"All right," said Dr Humphrey. "But it may be expensive."

"We can pay!" Mrs Brown assured him. "We just want our son back to how he was!"

Chapter Six

Before long Dr Humphrey arrived.
Murray was busy sweeping the
driveway.

They prised the broom from
Murray's hand and took him
inside.

Dr Humphrey sat Murray on the
sofa and started the reversal
treatment.

It took three and a half hours.
The doctor mopped his brow and
led Murray over to Mr and Mrs
Brown.

"OK, he's back to how he was,"
Dr Humphrey told them. "Just a
normal messy youngster."

And he was. Murray was every bit
as messy as before (if not a little
more so.)

Mr and Mrs Brown were delighted. The doctor took his fee, which was ninety-seven pounds this time. Then he left for his next clean-up-forever-reversal appointment.

Chapter Seven

Mr and Mrs Brown felt it was
money well spent. They loved to
watch Murray slouch around
the house.

They loved to watch him rest his feet on the furniture.

They loved to watch him drink
straight from the can, and eat
straight from the fridge.

They loved to watch him leave his
clothes all over the bedroom floor.

They took Murray round the
neighbourhood.
"We've got one like that at home,"
sighed Mr and Mrs Potter.

They took Murray to visit
relations.
"He's just like he should be at
his age," said Auntie Pat.
Everyone nodded. And Mr and
Mrs Brown were proud of him.